THE CHERRY TREE BUCK

TREE BUCK

and Other Stories

BY
ROBIN
MOORE

Alfred A. Knopf New York

TO THE MEMORY
OF MY GRANDFATHER,
CHALMER GROVE MOORE

Library of Congress Cataloging-in-Publication Data

Moore, Robin. The cherry tree buck and other stories / by Robin Moore ;
illustrated by Kees deKiefte.
p. cm.
Summary: A series of stories describes the tall tale adventures of a boy and his grandfather
with some of the creatures living near their home in central Pennsylvania.
ISBN 0-679-85641-2 (trade)
[1. Grandfathers—Fiction. 2. Animals—Fiction. 3. Pennsylvania—Fiction.
4. Humorous stories.]   I. Title.
PZ7.M78766Gr   1995   94-19479   [Fic]—dc20

Manufactured in the United States of America
10 9 8 7 6 5 4 3 2 1

CONTENTS

Introduction

I learned about the woods from my grand-father.

From the time I was old enough to hold a fishing pole, my grandfather and I spent every spare moment outdoors, enjoying whatever the wind and weather had to offer.

In those days, our part of Pennsylvania was still pretty wild. We could see black bear and wild turkey from the back porch. We could pick blueberries and collect mushrooms. We could drink right out of the streams and walk through the hills all day without seeing another person.

Sometimes we would wander off the familiar trails and plunge into the deepest, tangliest part of the thicket, just to see what was there. Sometimes we would sit quietly on the banks of a stream or at the edge of a meadow, waiting with watchful eyes. And sometimes, when we were very lucky, we would get a glimpse of the natural world that remains hidden to most people.

Some of the things we saw were, literally, incredible. Whenever we tried to tell our family or friends, they'd accuse us of pulling their legs. After a while we just kept quiet.

It's been nearly forty years since my grandfather died, and I think it's time to tell about our adventures. I once asked him, "What's the secret to telling a good story?"

He grinned. "No secret to it at all. Just start with the facts and go on from there...."

THE CHERRY TREE BUCK

TREE BUCK

and Other Stories

The Cherry Tree Buck

When I was a boy growing up in the mountains of central Pennsylvania, my grandfather used to take me deer hunting up in the woods behind our house.

We went every year in the first weeks of December, after the leaves had fallen but before the first snow, while the yellowed cornstalks still stood in the fields like a pale army rustling in the wind.

My grandfather was an old-fashioned

kind of person. He never took much interest in modern hunting equipment. Year after year, all through the 1950s and 1960s, he took me hunting with the same rifle: an old flintlock muzzle-loading gun that my great-grandfather had owned many years before I was born.

In all the years we went hunting together, we had never gotten a deer. But we were never discouraged. We knew that some year something miraculous would happen.

And one year a miracle did happen. Or I guess it was a miracle. You can judge for yourself....

We set off early one morning to climb the mountainside and wait by a deer trail, hoping to catch a glimpse of a big buck.

But we were no sooner settled than we realized that we had made a terrible mistake. We had the rifle and some gunpowder, but we had forgotten to bring any bullets.

We felt pretty stupid—there we were, all the way up in the woods, with no bullets.

Fortunately, my grandmother had packed us a paper bag of cherries.

We were sitting underneath a big hemlock tree, eating the cherries and spitting out the pits, when I had an inspiration. I looked down at the cherry seeds in my hand.

"Grandpa," I said, "couldn't we use these for bullets?"

My grandfather nodded. "It's sure worth a try," he said.

My grandfather dropped a charge of gunpowder down the barrel of the rifle. Then he wrapped the cherry seed in a little cloth patch and used his ramrod to shove it into the barrel. He poured a spot of priming powder in the flash pan and snapped it shut. We were ready.

Just then we heard a rustling sound up ahead, and a magnificent buck stepped out onto the trail. He was a "six-point," meaning that he had six pointed tines on each antler—a very impressive rack for a Pennsylvania deer.

My grandfather raised the rifle and sighted in on the deer's chest. He held his breath and squeezed the trigger.

There was a shower of sparks, a loud explosion—and then the air was filled with blue smoke. The rifle had gone off just fine.

But when the smoke cleared I could see the deer standing there, seemingly unhurt. He was shaking his head from side to side, as if stunned by the explosion.

I noticed that the hair on top of the deer's head was ruffed up, and I realized what had happened. My grandfather had aimed high. Instead of going into the chest, the hard cherry seed had flown through the air and stuck in the skin on top of the deer's head!

Finally, the deer came to his senses and ran off.

We both thought it was one of strangest things we had ever seen.

The next year, in the spring, we were out walking around in that same part of the woods when we saw something even stranger.

We looked up the mountainside and there was a cherry tree in full blossom, walking down the trail toward us.

I looked and I could see: It was that deer, with a cherry tree about three feet tall growing out of the top of his head!

I realized what had happened.

That seed must have been stuck under his skin all winter and in the spring some rain probably fell on him—so, naturally, the little tree just sprouted right up!

A little later in the season he got about a dozen red cherries on the tree, hanging in between his antlers.

We decided to protect the deer because, even in central Pennsylvania, we very rarely get a deer with a cherry tree growing out of the top of his head. So we posted "No Hunting" signs all over our land, and the local hunters respected that.

That deer grew up pretty well.

And the cherry tree grew pretty well, too. It got to be about fourteen feet tall. And you could get a bushel of cherries just by following the deer around and picking up what he dropped.

We had a ball watching that deer in every season.

Then one year, during the hunting season, a terrible thing happened. My grandfather and I were inside the house early one morning, eating breakfast, when we heard a sound in the woods behind our cornfield. It was the sharp, earsplitting crack of a modern rifle.

We looked out our window to see a hunter walking out of our woods and into our cornfield.

We put on our coats and walked out there to tell him he wasn't allowed to be on our land. But as we were walking through the dried cornstalks we saw something dark lying in the corn rows.

When we got closer, I could see it was the cherry tree buck.

I never saw my grandfather lose his temper like he did that day. He stormed through the dried corn and located the hunter just as he was coming to the edge of the fields. I could see that he wasn't from around here; he was one of those sportsmen who drive up from the cities every fall with the price tags still hanging from their hunting clothes. My grandfather grabbed him by the scruff of his neck and the seat of his pants and walked him off our land.

When he came back, my grandfather examined the deer. But it was no use.

The deer was dead.

Normally, when we came across a road kill or when someone gave us a deer he had shot and didn't want, we would give the meat to my grandmother and she would use it for steaks and soups and stews. My grandfather would tan the skin for moccasins and hunting bags. And we would find a use for just about every part of the deer: tying fishing flies from the tail hairs and making whistles from the leg bones.

But we didn't do that this time. Instead my grandfather got two shovels from his workshed. We dug a hole in the center of the cornfield and buried the deer with his legs folded under him, his nose facing west, and that cherry tree sticking up out of the ground.

It was worth a try.

The following spring the tree gave us a beautiful crop of cherries.

Early in the season, I walked out with my stepladder and bucket to pick the first cherries of the year. I set up my ladder and climbed into the upper branches, dropping the cherries into my bucket.

Then I made the mistake of popping one into my mouth.

"Ow!" I yelled. I had bitten into something sharp.

My grandfather came running over. "What's the problem?" he asked.

I fished around in my mouth and pulled out two little twiggy-looking things.

"I'm all right, Grandpa. I must have gotten

a sharp stem in my mouth," I said.

I reached up, picked another cherry, and slipped it into my mouth.

"Ow!" I hollered again. That hurt worse than the first time!

"Now what?" my grandfather said. "Is there something wrong with those cherries?"

Something had jabbed into my tongue. I reached into my mouth and pulled out two sharp curvy things.

Then I looked up into the cherry tree and realized what had happened: Every one of those little individual cherries had a tiny set of deer antlers in them!

"Well, I'll be—" my grandpa said. "That's amazing."

It *was* amazing. Year after year that tree bore us crops of cherries with little six-pointers in them. They were perfectly good cherries. The only problem was, by the time you had de-pitted and de-antlered them, it would take you all afternoon to get enough for a pie.

We still have a few of those miniature antlers around the house. We use them for toothpicks when company comes over.

As far as I know, that cherry tree is still growing in the center of our cornfield. And I hope it grows there a long, long time.

The Sawdust Bear

Back in the 1920s, thirty years before I was born, our part of Pennsylvania was a haven for black bears. They made their homes in the rocky crags of the mountains that surrounded our valley. Every now and then people would see bear tracks in the mud along the streams. Sometimes they would even see the bears in broad daylight, foraging for food.

Then one year, late in the fall, when my grandfather was barely twenty years old, he shot one of the biggest black bears ever taken in the Pennsylvania mountains. He didn't mean to shoot him. It was an accident. Grandpa had been out deer hunting with his old flintlock rifle when he stumbled across a black bear.

The bear charged; my grandfather fired.

The bear fell dead.

It took five men to drag the shaggy black carcass down out of the woods. People came from all over to see it. Bears are so elusive that, even in those days, there were many people in our town who had never seen one up close. The men spent the rest of the day skinning and butchering, doing a real careful job.

Herman Hemsley, one of the men who helped with the skinning, was a part-time taxidermist. He said he would stuff that bear for my grandfather so Grandpa could always remember his close brush with death.

My grandfather agreed. He could picture how magnificent that bear would look standing by the fireplace in the living room, its blue-black fur burnished by the firelight.

It took Herman three months, working evenings and weekends, to get that bear stuffed and mounted.

First he built a sturdy frame from stiff wire. Then he added contours by wrapping the frame with strips of cloth, layered with wood shavings and sawdust. Once the form was complete, he sewed the huge skin over it and added teeth, claws, and glass eyeballs. Then he mounted the whole thing on a heavy base made from solid oak.

I guess Herman wanted the bear to look fierce. So he stood him up on his hind legs, his mouth forever open in a silent roar, his paws extended in a threatening gesture.

Everyone agreed it was Herman's masterpiece, the highest form of the taxidermist's art.

One day, early in spring, a bunch of men loaded the bear into the back of my grandfather's pickup truck and drove it over to the house. This was back when the brick house was new. He and my grandmother had gotten married the year before and were just beginning to settle into the routine of life together.

When my grandmother saw the truck pull up, she came out onto the front porch and stood with her hands on her hips.

"I hope you're not thinking of bringing that thing into the house," she said.

Grandpa was momentarily stunned. "What are you talking about? Of course it's going in the house, right there by the fireplace in the living room."

My grandmother shook her head. "Oh, no, it's not," she said emphatically. "I'm not spending the next forty years sweeping up bear hair and dusting cobwebs off that thing!"

Grandpa threw his hands up in the air. "Well, where do you expect me to put it?"

My grandmother pointed to the shed behind the house, where my grandfather had his workshop. "Put it back there," she said.

"What? Have you lost your senses?" my grandfather shouted.

Herman spoke up, trying to reason with my grandma. "We can't put it in the shed," he explained. "This is a fine piece of taxidermy. It's gotta be stored under optimal conditions. If we put it out there, the fleas will lay their eggs in the bear's fur, the rats'll chew on his feet, and the field mice'll make nests in his ears!"

My grandmother planted her feet and crossed her arms across her chest. "You men can talk all you want. That bear is not coming in this house."

Still, my grandfather was determined. Ignoring my grandma, he made the men unload the bear and carry it up the front steps and onto the porch.

But the shaggy beast wouldn't fit through the front door. And as Grandma pointed out, he wouldn't stand up in the living room either; the ceiling was too low.

So, in the end, they followed my grandmother's wishes. They carried the bear out to the shed and placed him in the corner of my grandfather's workshop, where he stood on his hind legs for thirty years, until I came along.

Herman Hemsley was right. The shed wasn't a very good place to store the sawdust bear. The fleas ate at him until his ears grew bare and his hair fell off in big clumps. The mice nibbled on his feet, and squirrels bored in through his ear holes and stored nuts in him for the winter.

But I loved the sawdust bear. To me he was always immense, powerful, and full of strange magic. I was never afraid of him, like the other kids were. It's true, his posture was threatening, his claws were massive and wickedly sharp, his teeth looked powerful and dangerous. But the one thing the taxidermist couldn't change was the expression on the bear's face. He never looked fierce to me. Instead he looked kind of puzzled and maybe a little sad. Those glass eyeballs gave his gaze a faraway look. From where that great bear stood, he could look out the window over my grandfather's workbench. His gaze always seemed to be fixed on something beyond the cornfields and the pumpkin patches, up in the mountains where he had come from so long ago.

Many times I wondered if the sawdust bear felt confined in the workshop, away from the sunlight and the wind and the smells of the open air. But a secret part of me was glad that he was there, always waiting for me when I came to visit.

Then one day, when I was about ten years old, a strange thing happened.

It started innocently enough. My grandfather and I were out in the shed. It was a brisk winter's day and Gramps had a crackling fire going in the wood stove. He was sitting on his stool at the workbench, rewiring a toaster for my grandmother. I was poking around in the back of the shed, going through an old chest of drawers.

I opened a small wooden drawer. There,

in the weak light, I could make out a pile of strange objects. They were made of pieces of wood and hollowed-out bones, tied together with scraps of leather and twine.

"Grandpa," I said, "what are these?"

My grandfather put down his tools and came over to see what I'd found.

He smiled. "Why, Robin, I forgot I still had those. They've probably been sitting in this drawer for thirty years."

"What are they?"

"Well, they're animal calls. This one's a mallard duck call. And this one here is a turkey call, for spring gobbler season. And this"—he held up a strange-looking thing made from a hollowed-out deer antler with a piece of birch bark threaded through it—"this is a female bear grunt call."

"What's it for?"

"For hunting bear! You blow in the end of

it and it imitates the sound of a female bear grunting in the mating season. That way, it calls the male right to you."

"When is the bear mating season?"

"Well, Robin, it's just about now. For the next month or so, those females will be calling to the males. Of course, there aren't nearly as many bears as there were back in the old days, so it's harder and harder for the bears to find a mate."

"How about that female we saw in the woods last summer? Would she be making calls like this?"

"Well, sure, I guess so."

"Grandpa! Let's use this call to go up in the woods and find some bears."

My grandfather shook his head. "No, Robin, that'd be way too dangerous. You shouldn't be messing with the bears during mating season. They can get real ornery this time of year. Now let's put these things away and forget we ever talked about it."

Sadly I placed the animal calls back in the drawer and slid it closed.

But I just couldn't get the thought of that female bear grunt call out of my mind. I had to hear what it sounded like and, more important, I had to see if it really worked.

In the days that followed, I hatched a plan. I would take the call and sneak into the woods, making my way up the mountainside to a clearing where, the summer before, we'd seen a black bear and her cub. To be safe, I would climb a tree. Then, with all the proper precautions made, I would blow the call and wait to see what would happen.

A dozen times I almost told my grandfather, hoping that he would join me in my adventure. Deep inside I suspected that he was as curious as I was but was afraid of what my grandmother might say if she found out that we had snuck out to spend time with the bears.

So the next Saturday morning, when no one else was up, I crept out to my grandfather's workshop, slipped the call into my pocket, and headed for the mountainside. In a half hour I was up a tree at the edge of the clearing, with the call pressed to my lips.

I blew softly at first, not knowing what kind of noise it would make. What came out was a pretty impressive grunting sound. I blew again, harder this time.

All the while I had my eyes on the clearing, hoping to catch a glimpse of a black bear.

It didn't take me long to learn the nuances of that bear call. I discovered that if I buzzed my lips as I blew, I could create an interesting tremolo effect. Before long I was giving a little concert of bear grunts from my perch in the tree.

As the calls became louder, they echoed off the sides of the mountain. The sound seemed to fill the woods, ricocheting across the hills and drifting down into the valley.

At last, I saw a bear approaching. A big male lumbered into the clearing on all fours, his nose held high. I grew a little afraid and stopped blowing calls. I just sat in the crook of the tree limb and watched him.

After a few moments my fear subsided. But I was still in awe of the tremendous power that rippled under the bear's shaggy coat as he moved about the clearing.

Fascinated, I leaned out farther and farther onto the branch, not realizing what I was doing. All that mattered to me was that I get a good look at that bear.

It was while I was straining to keep him in view that I heard a sharp crack. The branch had given way beneath me! I dropped fifteen feet and landed in a pile of soft leaves.

I wasn't hurt, but the sound of the falling branch had alerted the bear. He turned and looked at me for what seemed like a very long time. He wrinkled his brow as if he was trying to figure out who I was.

At that moment I was genuinely afraid, and sorry that I had done such a stupid thing.

The bear surveyed me for a long time. I held as still as I could, pretending to be a tree stump. The bear dropped on all fours and casually walked to me. When he was within a few feet he stopped and sniffed me. His black nostrils were less than a yard from my face. The moisture from his breath formed a cloud that drifted in my direction, bringing me his terrifying animal scent.

I braced myself for the swipe of a razor-sharp paw, or the headlong charge that I knew could come at any instant.

But it did not come.

Instead the bear rumbled deep in his chest, making a great groaning growl that seemed to shake the earth underneath me. Then he turned and was gone, loping heavily up the mountainside and into the cover of the trees.

I waited until I could no longer hear the sound of his paws on the leafy trail. Then I pulled myself to my feet and ran back to the house on shaky legs. I had been terrified, and I knew that what I had done was stupendously foolish. But what an adventure! I had called up a wild black bear, come face to face with the brute, and lived to tell the tale!

But as I neared my grandfather's house, I realized that I couldn't tell the tale. Who would I tell? My grandfather would be mad at me for disobeying. My grandmother would be furious at me for risking my life. My friends would never believe me.

This was the bittersweet irony of it: I had had a great adventure and I couldn't tell anyone about it! I decided that I would slip into the workshop, put the call into its drawer, and never mention anything to anyone.

But when I got down to the workshop, I noticed something strange. The shed door was standing wide open. I knew I had closed it when I left, and my grandfather would never leave it open.

"Maybe it was the wind," I said to myself. I stepped inside and swung the door closed behind me.

But when I looked into the half-darkness of the shed, I couldn't believe what I saw. The sawdust bear was gone!

In the corner where the bear used to stand, nothing remained but the heavy wooden base—and a double trail of sawdust going out the door and up toward the mountainside.

Then I realized what had happened. That female bear grunt call had been so effective it had even rekindled the passions of a bear that had been stuffed for thirty years! The sawdust bear was out roaming the mountain-side, looking for a mate. No wonder he hadn't been interested in me.

Now there was no way out of it. Later that morning I told my grandfather the whole story.

He couldn't believe it at first. I took him out to the workshop and showed him the sawdust trail, but he was still doubtful. Even after we tracked the bear a ways up into the hills, Grandpa found my story hard to believe.

Then, a few days later, one of the workers down at the local sawmill told Grandpa and me that he had spotted a large black bear prowling around the sawdust piles.

"It was the strangest thing," the man said.

"That bear sat down on his haunches and began using his paws to shovel sawdust into his mouth. A sawdust-eating bear. I've never seen anything like it!"

My grandfather and I looked at each other. We knew what was happening. The bear was just swallowing a little extra sawdust to make up for the stuffing he had lost during his dash to freedom.

I like to think the bear did find his freedom. I like to think that he made it up into the mountains, to that place he had been looking at through the window for all those years. I'd like to think that he heard the grunt of a real female bear and that he found a mate and lived out his life in peace and safety, as a bear should.

My grandfather and I never told anybody what really happened to the sawdust bear. We said we had hauled him out to the town dump and thrown him down a sinkhole with a bunch of other things that no one wanted anymore: old washing machines and broken bicycles and cardboard boxes.

But I like to think that's he still up in the mountains, somewhere. And if he is, I hope we never find him.

The Diamondback Rattlesnake

There is nothing more pitiful than a toothless rattlesnake.

Grandpa and I saw one down at the Black Moshanon Nature Center one hot summer afternoon. The snake was curled up, coil on coil, in a square wire cage on a table in the far corner. We walked over and had a look at him.

My grandfather knew the naturalist, a young fellow named Herbert who used to pump gas at our neighborhood filling station. He was a gawky, awkward kid with no mechanical ability whatsoever, so his future at the service station was limited. But then he found this new job, for less pay but more prestige, at the local park. He got to wear a uniform and a badge and the tourists would call him "Ranger Herb," which pleased him to no end.

"Well, Herb," my grandfather said, "looks like you got yourself a diamondback here."

"Yep," Herb said, coming out of his office. "That's a real *Crotalus adamanteus.*"

Herb always did enjoy showing off.

"How'd you get him?" I asked.

"Oh, one of the game protectors brought him in. He was living under the porch down at the visitors center. The park director wanted to kill him but then I stepped in. I said I thought it would be much smarter to have him defanged and use him here at the nature center as an educational tool."

Herb seemed very pleased with himself.

"You mean he can't bite anyone?" I asked.

"Nope. Look here." Herb got a stick and poked it through the wire cage, touching the slumbering snake on the snout. The reptile lazily opened his mouth in a wide yawn. Sure enough, the two front fangs were missing. When the snake closed his mouth again he looked like a toothless old man.

"If he hasn't got fangs, how does he hunt and eat?" Grandpa asked.

"Oh, his hunting days are over," Herb said. "I catch field mice and feed him one every couple days."

"What does he do," I asked, "gum it to death?"

"Nah, he just swallows it whole. Then he lies there and digests it, slowly."

My grandfather and I both shook our heads. "Pitiful," Grandpa said.

I'll admit that, up until that moment, I had

never had much sympathy for rattlesnakes. Like most everybody, I was afraid of them and tried my best to stay out of their way. But there was something about this snake and its situation that saddened me. The rattler opened his bleary eyes and looked at us absently. His tail flicked once or twice, but the rattle sounded feeble and halfhearted.

"Will the fangs ever grow back?" I asked.

"Normally they do," Herb said, "but for some reason, that hasn't happened to this fella. I guess he'll just be toothless his whole life. But, in the meantime, it's lucky for us. The Boy Scout troop that meets in here has been working on its reptile studies merit badge, and the boys have had a great time handling the snake and observing him."

"Think he'll hibernate here for the winter?" I asked.

"Won't have a chance to," Herbert said.

"The nature center closes at the end of the summer and I gotta go back to the filling station. I'll probably just release him in the woods out back and let nature take its course."

"What do you mean?" I asked.

"What Herbert means," my grandfather put in, "is that he'll starve to death. Without a set of fangs he'll be as helpless in the woods as a newborn babe."

"Well, Robin," Herb said, "you gotta understand. These things happen in nature. Survival of the fittest and all that."

"Except for one thing," Grandpa said. "It was you, not nature, that decided to take out his fangs."

"Maybe so," Herb said, "but at least the Boy Scouts got to learn something from the whole thing. I always say, if we don't teach these kids to respect the environment, where is our world gonna be?"

Grandpa and I cast sidelong glances at each other.

"Grandpa," I said, "couldn't we take that snake—"

He held up his hand. "No. Don't even start thinking that way. Your grandmother would skin me alive if I brought home a rattlesnake."

"She wouldn't have to know," I assured him. "We could keep him out in the work-shop. She never comes out there."

"But how would we feed him? And what would we do when winter comes?"

When my grandfather started grumbling like that, I knew I was winning him over.

"Besides," I said, sweetening the deal, "you know that wood-carving project you started and never finished? The one with the rattle-snake coiled around a tree limb? This way you'd have a live model to work from."

I could see that I had him.

"Well, maybe you got a point there," Grandpa conceded. "All right, we'll give it a try. Herbert, if that rattler doesn't grow a new set of fangs by the end of the summer, we'll take him off your hands."

Herb shrugged. "Suits me."

We stopped in a few times during the summer to check on the snake. Each time Herb assured us he was as toothless as ever.

Just before the Labor Day weekend, Herb called us to come over and get our snake. He said we could take the wire cage with us.

It was easy sneaking him into the workshop. My grandmother didn't suspect a thing, and we were sure she would never discover our secret. She never came out to the workshop. She considered it a smelly, dangerous place and couldn't understand why we spent so much time out there. Grandma had even made my grandfather run a phone line from the house so she could call him for dinner without having to set foot in the workshop.

I made a mouse trap out of a metal bucket full of water and a block of wood, with cracked corn for bait, and fed the snake a steady diet of drowned mice.

The rattler was not a very exciting pet. He slept most of the time, curled up in his cage.

Then one morning something happened that changed all that.

I found my grandfather at his workbench, polishing something with a piece of steel wool. On the bench in front of him were several nature books, showing drawings and photographs of snakes with their fangs exposed.

Grandpa blew the dust off his work and held it under the workbench light.

"Well, Robin, what do you think?"

Between his thumb and forefinger was a slender, polished piece of bone.

"What is it?" I asked.

Gramps beamed. "It's an artificial fang. Here, look, I got two of 'em. I made them out of chicken bones from last night's dinner. Pretty realistic, huh?"

I looked back and forth from the illustrations to the fangs. I had to admit, they looked pretty authentic.

"They look great," I said, "but how are you gonna attach them?"

"Already thought of that. I figured I'd use that real strong instant-bonding glue I use to fix your grandmother's necklaces."

"But he really won't be able to use them, will he?"

"What? The necklaces?"

"No! The fangs."

"No, Robin, he won't. But I figure it'll just make him feel better about himself. Just like when I got my false teeth. Being toothless is a terrible thing. I know. I've been through it."

Grandpa reached into the wire cage, caught the snake right behind the head, and drew him out, laying him on the workbench. That snake thrashed around and whipped his tail in the air. He was surprisingly strong. But we finally managed to get him calmed down. Grandpa forced the snake's mouth open, and, working quickly, I put a dab of glue on the end of each fang and popped them in place against the roof of the snake's mouth. The glue dried instantly.

We put the snake back in the cage and watched.

At first the rattler just crawled around and around. But at last he settled down and seemed to be considering his new condition. I ran into the house and brought out Grandpa's hand-held shaving mirror, and we set it up so the snake could see himself.

The rattler opened his mouth wide and turned his head from side to side, checking himself out from every angle. You don't have to know much about rattlesnakes to know that that snake was pleased. Instead of lying there in a miserable coil, he held his head high, flicking his forked tongue and shaking his rattle like crazy.

Grandpa opened the cage door and the snake slithered out into the room, gracefully negotiating the piles of wood and boxes of tools, flicking his tongue at everything.

Grandpa and I were pretty pleased with

ourselves. We sat and watched that snake for quite a while, just enjoying the poetry of his movements as he made his way across the wooden floor of the workshop.

It was fun watching him, but after a while the sound of his rattle began to get on my nerves. It was the same pattern over and over.

All of a sudden, my grandfather sprang from his stool. "No," he said. "It can't be..."

"What?"

"Shh...listen: Dah...Dit Dit Dit Dit ...Dit-Dah..." It was as if my grandfather was speaking some strange foreign language.

"What is it?" I insisted.

"Morse code," my grandfather said.

Morse code! I didn't know much about Morse code except that my grandfather had been a telegraph operator during World War I and that he had sent thousands of messages across France and Germany using this system of dots and dashes, long and short sounds.

"Listen," he said. "Here it comes again: Dah...that's one dash, that's a *T*...Dit Dit Dit Dit...four dots, that's an *H*...Dit-Dah, that's *A*...Dah-Dit, *N*...Dah-Dit-Dah, *K*...Dit Dit Dit, *S*."

My grandfather and I looked at each other in astonishment. It couldn't be a coincidence. That snake knew Morse code and was trying to communicate with us!

We listened to the message again and, sure enough, it was the same.

"How did this snake learn Morse code?" Grandpa asked.

"Well," I said, laughing, "why don't you ask him?"

My grandfather knew instantly what I was thinking. He grabbed a metal spoon from his workbench and sat cross-legged on the wooden floor in front of the snake. The rattler wasn't rattling anymore; he was just looking at my grandfather with expectant eyes.

Tapping with the spoon on the wooden floorboards, Grandpa rapped out a slow series of Dits and Dahs, saying, "Greetings, friend. How did you learn Morse code?"

Once he had finished, the snake stared at my grandfather for several seconds. For the first time, I noticed a change in the snake's eyes. They were not just dark dots anymore. Within the darkness of its gaze, a keen intelligence was at work.

The snake began rattling. I watched in amazement as my grandfather grabbed a pencil and pad of yellow paper and began writing furiously. Letter by letter, word by word, an astonishing story developed.

After being captured and suffering the indignity of being defanged, the snake was sure he was going to die. But as time went

on, he accepted Herb's mice as food and settled into an impossibly boring period of
captivity. The nature center was quiet,
except when the Boy Scouts had their meetings there. Then the room would be filled
with shouting, whooping boys, all of whom
wanted to handle the snake and poke things
into his mouth. He was repelled by the
whole idea.

But one thing about those Scout meetings
did fascinate him. Although snakes cannot
hear as we do, they are very sensitive to
vibrations through the ground. The Boy
Scouts used the long table his cage was on
for their Morse code practice. They had set
up two telegraph keys on the table and
would tap out messages to one another endlessly.

Since he was a captive audience to the
vibrations coming through the table, the
bored reptile seized on the intellectual chal-

lenge of deciphering the code. By the end of summer, he was an ace at it. He had tried to communicate a few times, using his rattle to summon a response from the boys. But they were as thick as stumps and never paid any attention to him. So the snake waited for an opportunity to communicate with some more receptive humans. And when Grandpa gave him the fangs, he thought that maybe his chance had come.

After Grandpa read me the message, he tapped out, "Good boy."

To which the snake answered: "I'm a female. You can call me Sheba."

So we did.

In the days that followed, we had many fascinating conversations with the snake. Sheba insisted, for instance, that humans have no reason to be afraid of snakes and that snakes have a lot to teach. For one thing, Sheba said, a snake can shed its skin, moving on to a new life and leaving the old worn-out life behind.

I remembered reading in one of my history books that the ancient Egyptians had honored and revered snakes for just that reason. The book had said that snakes were the symbol of rebirth and regeneration and were highly respected.

Sheba certainly did change my ideas about snakes, and about a lot of other things, too. Moving with painstaking slowness, letter by letter, my grandfather filled two writing tablets with messages taken from the snake. I still have them somewhere. Maybe I'll make them into a book someday.

Then a strange thing happened. It was toward the end of summer, on a hot day in August. I had just finished breakfast at my parents' house when the phone rang. It was my grandfather on the other end, but I could hardly hear him. He was coughing and trying to talk, but he sounded as if he were a million miles away.

"Grandpa?" I said. "Grandpa? Are you there?"

There was no answer. Then, through the receiver, I heard a strange kind of buzzing, and I realized it was the rattlesnake! By now I knew Morse code pretty well myself. I concentrated on the sound of the rattles coming through the phone lines. Dit Dit Dah-Dit, *F*...Dit Dit, *I*...Dit-Dah-Dit, *R*...Dit, *E*. FIRE!

I looked out the window onto my grandparents' property and saw smoke billowing from the open door of the workshop!

I raced out the back door, sprinted across the yard, and burst into the workshop. My grandfather was sprawled on the floor, one hand over his heart, his face as pale as moonlight. I could see that he had fallen and knocked over a kerosene lantern. A small fire was crackling in a pile of scrap wood by the workbench. The snake lay in a coil by my grandfather's head, its tail near the receiver of the phone.

I took all this in with one glance. Quickly I filled a bucket with water from the big sink in the corner and sloshed it onto the burning wood. The fire died instantly. Kneeling by my grandfather, I saw that he was unconscious but still breathing. I snatched up the phone and called the local ambulance. By the time I hung up, I could already hear the siren.

It was my grandfather's first heart attack. A minor one, the doctor said, but still serious enough to keep him off his feet for a week or so. By the end of August my grandfather was fully recovered.

Once Grandpa came home from the hospital, we told my grandmother about the snake. We wanted her to know how Sheba had saved Grandpa's life.

"Well," Grandma said, "I never thought I'd be thankful to a rattlesnake. But I guess I am."

I didn't have much time for the snake while Grandpa was getting back on his feet. Even though she had been kind of a heroine, I guess I was so worried about Grandpa that I neglected to feed Sheba or spend much time with her.

Then one day I walked into the workshop and saw that Sheba was gone. As I was searching for a sign of the brave snake, I saw something light and papery stuck between the stones of the foundation. I knelt and carefully drew it out. It was a perfect replica of Sheba, right down to the eyes and the mouth. She had shed her skin, and shed this life, leaving behind this exquisite reminder.

I walked outside and held the skin up to the sky. Hundreds of diamonds glittered in the sunlight.

I smiled, thinking about this cold-blooded reptile who had taught me so much. The thought occurred to me that if a snake could learn Morse code and communicate with humans, maybe we could try to learn some of the animals' languages, taking just a few short steps in their direction, so that the day would come, just like in the old storybooks, when animals and humans would speak the same language.

The Heart of an Eagle

If there was anyone who loved birds more than my grandfather, it had to be my uncle Cliff.

Clifford even looked a little like a bird. He was tall and thin and bald on top, with a long neck and a big Adam's apple that stuck out above his shirt collar. He and my aunt Sarah raised chickens and turkeys and Canada geese on their farm down in Woodward.

One summery day Grandpa and I drove

down the valley to pay them a visit.

Their farm was small but well kept, with a neat barn and outbuildings, a barnyard for the animals, and a little jewel of a pond.

When we pulled in, Cliff waved to us from his chair on the front porch.

"Good to see you boys!" he hollered. "What brings you down this way?"

Grandpa grinned. "Just came for a change of scenery. Why don't you show us around the place?"

Cliff proudly showed us the work he had done on the outside of the barn and a few extra chicken coops he had added.

As we were walking by one of the chicken coops, he motioned to us.

"I want you boys to come over and have a look at this," he said.

I hooked my fingers in the chicken wire and peered into the dusty enclosure. I strained my eyes in among the sea of milling, clucking hens. Toward the back, partly hidden by shadows, I saw a bird that was bigger and darker than the rest, scratching in the dirt.

"He looks like a crow," I said.

Grandpa laid a hand on my shoulder. "Look again. That's no crow, Robin. That's a sure-enough bald eagle!"

I had seen bald eagles before, riding the wind currents along the mountain ridges. But this bird didn't look like any eagle I'd ever seen.

"Where are his markings?" I asked. My grandfather had taught me to pick out the eagles by the white markings on the head and tail.

"He hasn't got his adult plumage yet," Clifford answered. "He's an immature male, all dusky-colored now."

My grandfather just shook his head in amazement.

"I've never seen anything like it," he said. "I never thought I'd live to see an eagle in a chicken coop. Talk about letting the fox in the henhouse. Aren't you worried that he'll make a meal of your chickens?"

"No, I'm not."

"Why not?"

Clifford sighed. "Because that eagle doesn't know he's an eagle. He thinks he's a chicken."

"How come?" I asked.

"Well, it all started about a year ago. I got a call from a family that lives up near Bald Eagle Mountain, saying that they found a bald eagle's nest, full of eggs. But they didn't see an adult eagle anywhere around. Naturally, they were afraid something might have happened to the mama. So they called me to see if I could save the eggs.

"I drove over to have a look and, sure enough, it was a bald eagle's nest. I called Ralph Hebner down at the state police barracks and wouldn't you know, they had just arrested some durned fool who had shot a mature female eagle with a .22 rifle, for the fun of it."

My grandfather just shook his head in disgust.

"What'd you do?" I asked.

"Well," Clifford said, "only one thing I could do. We watched that nest for another day, just to make sure. Then I put a ladder up that tree and collected those eggs. I brought 'em home and put 'em underneath one of my chickens. I figured it was worth a try.

"As it turned out, only one of those eggs hatched. That little eaglet was the most pitiful-looking thing you ever saw: all pink and bald-headed and wrinkled. But my hens didn't seem to notice. They treated him just like the other chicks and raised him as a chicken. He grew up around chickens. I guess being a chicken is all he knows."

My grandfather shook his head. "That *is* pitiful," he said. "That bird shouldn't be cooped up with these hens. He should be up in the mountains somewhere, flyin' around."

"*I* know that," Clifford said. "But when I let him out of the coop, all he does is wander around and peck in the dirt like a chicken. That's why I'm showing you this bird right now. I figure you might have some fresh ideas."

I looked up at my uncle. "You mean you want us to teach this eagle how to fly?" I asked.

"I wish you could," Clifford said, winking at my grandfather. "He eats about five pounds of seed a week and he hasn't laid me an egg yet."

My grandfather laughed at Clifford's joke, then turned to me. "What do you say, Robin? Should we give it a try?"

I shrugged. "Why not? But how?"

Grandpa scratched the back of his neck and stared down at the ground for what seemed like a long time. Suddenly he looked up.

"Robin, you know those leather work-gloves on the floor of the pickup?"

"Yeah."

"Go get 'em. I got an idea."

I fetched the gloves. They were the ones my grandfather wore when he ran his chain saw. They were stained with oil and flecked with sawdust. But they were made from thick cowhide, with stiff cuffs. Looking a little like a gladiator going into the arena, Grandpa pulled on the gloves and nodded toward the coop.

"Clifford, you get that door open for me."

"What are you gonna do?"

"Go in there and bring that eagle out. We can't teach him a thing as long as he's amongst all those chickens."

Clifford opened the door and my grandfather slipped past him, stepping into the shadowy coop.

From our side of the wire I watched as my grandfather made his way carefully through the milling chickens toward the back of the coop, where the eagle was feeding at a bin of seed. Ever so slowly he moved up to the eagle. Then he crouched down and placed his gloved hand on the ground. This strange behavior aroused the eagle's curiosity. The eagle pecked at the glove once or twice.

My grandfather started speaking in a low, comforting voice, the kind he might use in talking to a small child.

"You're a fine bird," Grandpa said. "You deserve better than this. You don't deserve to be in a barnyard. Come on, boy, I'll show you some open sky."

The eagle watched him for several moments, curious but cautious. Then he surprised us all by stepping onto the glove, gripping my grandfather's fingers with his talons, and allowing himself to be lifted up and carried out of the coop.

"That was easy," Grandpa said.

Once he was outside, I half expected the eagle to take off. But he didn't. The bird just balanced there on my grandfather's hand, looking around.

I got my first really good look at him then. The curving hook of his beak and the powerful grip of his talons made him look dangerous. But he didn't act dangerous. He just sat there, like a chicken.

Clifford latched the door. "Now what?"

"Well," Grandpa said, "the way I figure it, this bird's problem is pretty simple. He doesn't know who he is. He's grown up thinking he's a chicken. He's got the habits of a chicken, it's true.

"But there's one thing those chickens

couldn't change about him—he's got the heart of an eagle. Once he realizes that, his true nature will take over. Then he'll just spread his wings and take that first leap. Nature will do the rest."

"Sounds good to me," Clifford said. "Now all we gotta do is convince this bird."

My grandfather held the eagle up high, so the wind could catch his wings. Then he starting talking to him.

"I know you think you're a chicken," Grandpa said, "but you're not. You're an eagle. All you gotta do is flap those big wings!"

But that eagle just sat there, his feathers ruffling in the wind.

Clifford stood with his hands in his pockets, leaning against the side of the barn.

"This is never gonna work," he said.

Then my grandfather had another idea.

"The hayloft," he said.

"What?" I said.

"You heard me! What we need is some elevation. Clifford, can you get that second-story loft door open?"

"Well, sure, but I don't think he's gonna—"

"Don't you worry about what he is or isn't gonna do. You just get that door open."

Clifford knew better than to stand in my grandfather's way when he was working on an idea. I had seen my grandfather like this many times, when something in nature especially caught his attention.

Clifford and Grandpa went in the barn and took the steps to the loft. While Grandpa held the bird, Clifford swung the loft door open. My grandfather kicked out two bales of hay and had me scatter them on the ground to break the eagle's fall.

"Now, Robin, you stay down there and

keep an eye on things. I'm gonna toss this bird out into the air. Once he starts falling, he'll just naturally know what to do."

It was a bad idea.

My grandfather tossed the eagle into the air.

"Fly!" he shouted. "You're a gol-durned eagle! Start acting like it!"

I was hoping the bird would take off in a flurry of feathers and sail out across the cornfields, majestic and serene.

But he didn't. He dropped like a bucket of bricks and landed in the soft hay, looking around him as if to say, "What happened?"

I looked up at the two men leaning out the hayloft door. Clifford just shook his head.

After all that, any other man would have been pretty discouraged, but not Grandpa. He came up with a new idea.

When they came down from the loft he said, "This isn't getting us anywhere. This bird needs to learn something he can only get from other birds. He needs to be with his own kind. Boys, let's get in the truck and go for a ride."

"Where to?" I asked.

"Up to Bald Eagle."

I knew what my grandfather was thinking. Bald Eagle Mountain is the highest peak for miles around. An old state forest road winds up to the base. From there it's a short, steep climb to the top of the ridge. At the peak there's a rocky cliff face where we would sometimes sit for hours, watching the hawks and turkey vultures capering on the breezes. I knew that's where we were headed.

We drove the truck up as far as we could. Then the three of us set off up the mountainside, my grandfather in the lead, carrying the eagle in his gloved hand, then my uncle Clifford, then me following behind. I pulled the hood of my sweatshirt over my head. It was a windy day, a little cold, but the sky was clear and seemed to stretch out endlessly in every direction.

My grandfather was talking to the bird as we walked.

"You spend your whole life in a chicken coop," he was saying, "and you never get to see this much sky, all in one piece."

As we broke up through the trees and onto the rocky outcrop on top of the mountain, a full view of the valleys and ridges lay before us. From up there, the human world of roads and farms and cornfields seemed laughably small, like marks on a map spread at our feet.

Up on the mountaintop, in the world of limestone and hemlocks and sunshine, I felt as if my petty lowland vision had changed over into a sharper, clearer way of seeing. I swept my gaze in every direction, feasting on the lush sweep of the valley floor and the rolling, humped-back ranges of the Tuscarora Mountains, purple in the distant light.

The eagle was looking, too. He turned his head from side to side, taking it all in. The pupils of his eyes grew wider, and darker.

I realized then that a chicken would never have a view like this. A chicken lives on the ground and sees close. An eagle lives in the air and sees far. I thought that maybe, at that moment, the eagle was seeing with his eagle eyes for the first time. Maybe he was remembering who he was.

Then the wind came up, threatening to blow us off the mountain.

"It's a windy day for flying lessons," Clifford shouted.

My grandfather grinned.

"Don't seem to be bothering them," he said, pointing above us. High up, hundreds of feet over our heads, I could see hawks and turkey vultures riding the wind currents, gracefully turning the wind in their favor.

The eagle watched, too, with a strange look of concentration.

After several long moments, the eagle turned his beak into the wind and tentatively lifted his wings.

"They're your relatives," Grandpa said to the bird. "You're one of them. They're waiting for you."

Then, holding the eagle aloft, my grandfather did a dangerous thing. He walked up to the very edge of the cliff. I knew that it dropped sheer for two hundred feet from that spot. Once, when the air was still, I had lain there on my belly, peering over the edge. But on a windy day like this, a sudden gust could send a person plummeting down the cliff face and onto the cruel rocks below.

I tried to shout to my grandfather, telling him to be careful, but he couldn't hear me. Clifford and I slid as close as we dared to the edge. I could see that Uncle Cliff was as worried about Grandpa as I was.

But Grandpa didn't seem worried at all. He just walked to the edge of the cliff, planted his feet on the rock, and held that bird up in the air.

"You're not a chicken," my grandfather shouted, "you're an eagle. And you weren't meant for the barnyard, you were meant for the snowpeaks and the sky..."

Then my grandfather dropped the eagle over the edge of the cliff.

I held on to Clifford and watched as the eagle fell, a pinwheel of feathers, tumbling down, down.

But just when the eagle seemed lost, a gust of wind came and caught him underneath the wings, lifting him up and away from the rocks below with the sound of a sword blade cutting the air. I watched as the wind lifted him up, his wings tilting, then straightening, flapping, once, twice. Then he glided out over the valley, sure and easy, just as if he had been flying for all of his natural-born days.

We watched the bird rise with the wind, higher and higher.

"You're an eagle," my grandfather shouted after him. "You're an eagle, by God. You're a sure-enough eagle!"

I'll never forget the look on my grandfather's face. His eyes were squinted against the sun and his mouth was formed into a toothy smile as he watched the eagle dancing on the wind. I'd never seen him so happy. At that moment I saw that he was a boy, no different from me, every fiber of his being filled with wonder and joy.

I glanced over at Clifford. He was smiling, too, shielding his eyes from the sun with his hand.

Then that eagle did a strange thing. He circled back our way and made one low pass right over our heads. For an impossibly long moment, he hung there in the breeze, looking down at us with shining black eyes. Then he tilted his wings slightly and slid off toward the western horizon in a great graceful arc. That was the last we saw of him.

Grandpa and Clifford and I walked slowly down the mountain and climbed into the truck. We didn't say much on the way home; I guess we didn't want to break the spell.

We had seen something set free. We had seen a creature discovering its true nature. But most of all, we had seen something worth remembering.

The Groundhog War

For as long as I could remember, my grandfather had grown vegetables—mostly beans, squash, and sweet corn—in a twenty-foot-square plot behind the house. It was enclosed in a shoulder-high wooden fence with a heavy gate and a secure metal latch that made a sharp click when it swung closed.

The garden was always a magical place to me. It gave us fresh food all summer long, it gave us fishing worms, but most of all, it gave us the pleasure of seeing things grow.

Every spring Grandpa liked to grow his own plants from seed in the workshop, and then, when the tender shoots were three or four inches high, he would transplant them into the garden.

One year early in May, my grandfather and I spent an entire afternoon planting the seedlings in straight neat rows in the rich black soil of the garden. We put in bean plants and muskmelons and a few tomato seedlings, then stood back to admire our work.

"You know, Robin," Grandpa said, wiping the dirt from his hands, "I've got a feeling that this is gonna be one of the best years we've ever had for the old garden."

He was wrong.

That night while we slept, a silent intruder entered our garden.

The next morning we took our time having breakfast. Then we put on our rubber boots and headed out to water the plants.

My grandfather stepped through the gate and took one look at the garden. I won't write down what he said. My grandmother had once told me that when she first met Grandpa, his everyday speech was peppered with curse words. In time, she had broken him of the habit. Or maybe not.

When I reached the garden gate, I stared in horror. Each of our tender vegetable seedlings had been neatly clipped off at the base, leaving row after row of ugly green stumps poking up through the dirt. And there, in the loose soil at the edge of the plot, were the unmistakable tracks of a groundhog.

"That darned whistle pig!" Grandpa exclaimed. He called groundhogs whistle pigs because they make a whistling sound through their teeth when they're alarmed.

It didn't take us long to find the spot where the groundhog had tunneled underneath the fence. We searched the edge of the woodline until we found the groundhog's hole, barely twenty yards from our garden fence.

My grandfather called down the hole, "You won't get away with this!"

There was no response from the occupant of the hole.

My grandfather turned and strode off down the hill. I followed close behind.

"Chicken wire," Grandpa said to me, his voice tense with anger.

"What?"

"Chicken wire" was all he would say. He kept repeating those words to himself, as if they had some strange magic power.

We got in the truck and drove to the hardware store, where Grandpa bought a hundred-foot roll of chicken wire. We spent the whole afternoon digging a foot-deep trench just inside the wooden fence. Then we nailed the chicken wire to the garden fence, burying the wire for a full foot underground.

"That'll keep him out," Grandpa said.

And it did, for a day or two, just long enough for us to buy a load of vegetable seedlings.

Grandpa hated to buy the plants, but it was too late to start his own again. So he swallowed his pride and bought a dozen flats of seedlings down at the gardening store. It took us most of an afternoon to get them in the ground.

That night the groundhog struck again, digging under the fence, under the chicken wire, and mowing down row after row of tender seedlings.

When my grandfather saw the destruction the next morning, he turned red and muttered a string of words that made my ears burn.

When he had calmed down a little, he turned to me.

"Now, Robin," he said, "I won't let this groundhog defeat us. Let's make a list of all the things we can do to protect our plants."

We went to town and came home with a truckload of supplies along with a fresh load of tender vegetable seedlings. The problem was, most people already had their plants in the ground and the selection was not very good. But we did the best we could, replacing what we had lost during the early, careless days of our campaign.

We put the new plants in the ground and set up our defenses.

We tried everything we could think of.

We tried hanging tin pie plates by strings from the fence so they would rattle in the wind and scare the groundhog.

We tried playing a transistor radio in the garden all night long.

We swept up clumps of hair from the floor of the local barber shop and scattered it all around the plants.

We tried dried blood and stale beer and mothballs.

Nothing worked.

Night after night, the groundhog made his raids, ravaging our plants.

By early June, only half our garden space was filled with living plants and we still had never caught a glimpse of the midnight marauder. My grandfather decided to go on the offensive.

He pointed to the woodline. "Let's go up there and have a talk with this whistle pig."

We positioned ourselves near the front entrance.

"I know you're down there," my grandfather said into the mouth of the hole, "probably sleeping off the last meal you had from my garden. But I want you to know that your days as a thief are just about over. I'm prepared to take drastic measures."

"But, Grandpa," I protested, "I don't want to hurt him."

My grandfather shook his head, "Neither do I. But the way I figure it, if we can get him to abandon this hole, maybe he'll go bother somebody else and leave our garden alone."

"How are we gonna do that?"

"The old-fashioned way. Let's get the hose."

It took us a while to string the hose all the way to the edge of the woods. My grandfather fed about six feet of garden hose into the earthy tunnel. Then he told me to run back to the house and turn on the water.

I had never realized how deep a groundhog's tunnel can be. It took almost a half hour for the hole to fill. We found the back entrance to the tunnel and kept an eye on it, but no one emerged. For a moment I feared that the groundhog was hiding out somewhere or, worse yet, that he and his brood had been trapped in the nether world of the tunnel and drowned.

Then, at the last possible moment, with water rising into the opening of the tunnel, the groundhog poked his head up from the main entrance and glanced around. But he could see that there was no escape. He swam up out of the muddy hole and scampered off into the woods, looking like a drowned rat. This was our first sight of the vegetable thief and, I have to say, I felt a little sorry for him.

We pulled out the hose and sealed both entrances by plugging them with big logs. Grandpa used a sledgehammer to drive the logs down into the mouth of the hole like corks in a bottle.

"That'll fix him," Grandpa said.

It did fix him for a few days, but not for long. The groundhog continued breaking into the garden and even managed to re-inhabit his home by digging a new entrance around the log barriers.

"Well," Grandpa said as he surveyed the pitiful remains of the seedlings, "I guess we just won't have a garden this year."

I had never seen him look so sad and defeated.

Then my grandmother came to the rescue. She saw an advertisement in one of her *Good Housekeeping* magazines for a product called "The Tunnel Tickler." It was expensive, about ten dollars. But, as she pointed out to Grandpa, he had already spent more money on the Groundhog War than a whole summerful of vegetables would cost.

So this was her way of having peace with dignity.

The postman brought the Tunnel Tickler on a Friday morning in June, in a plain brown wrapper. Grandma handed it to my grandfather, saying quietly, "Here, I got this for your groundhog."

My grandfather unwrapped it and looked it over. I could see that he was skeptical. It was a funny-looking thing: a metal stake with a tin cylinder on top that held four D-size flashlight batteries.

But as my grandfather read the directions, a triumphant smile spread across his face.

"This is brilliant," he said. "I should have thought of it myself."

"What's it do?" I asked.

"Well, the principle is really pretty simple. Inside this stake is a motor that vibrates the whole unit every minute or so. The vibration sends tremors through the subsoil that act on the burrowing animal's inner ear, sending him into a state of panic. On top of that, the gizmo emits an irritating buzzing sound every minute or so, which is supposed to scare the animals away. I figure we'll just bury it inside the garden, right by the plants."

"What plants?" I asked.

"Well, let's just put in some more plants and give it a try."

It was encouraging to see my grandfather regain his enthusiasm. For the third time, we replanted the garden. Then we drove the Tunnel Tickler into the ground and waited.

The next morning, when we walked out to the garden, we were delighted to see that the plants hadn't been touched. But the Tunnel Tickler was gone! We searched the entire garden, but there was no sign of the buzzing device.

Then, as we were puzzling over what to do next, we heard a faint, irritating buzzing sound coming from somewhere up in the woods. My grandfather and I looked at each other in disbelief.

At last, down on our hands and knees by the groundhog hole, we heard the buzzing from its very depths. Then we realized that the groundhog had taken the Tunnel Tickler down into the hole with him!

We got shovels and tried to retrieve our device. But it was no use; the soil was too hard and the tree roots were too thick.

It was a low ebb for us. We trailed back to the house and sat on the back porch, staring across the yard at the garden.

"Well," I said, "the garden isn't a complete failure. We did manage to get a few plants going."

I was right. Somehow the plants had matured and given us a pretty good crop of tomatoes, some beans, and a pitiful crop of lumpy squash. Even though the groundhog still dug his way in every night, his appetite wasn't as ravenous as before and there was plenty of food to go around. Each morning, it was part of our routine to take a shovel and fill in the tunnel the groundhog had made under the fence the night before. I suppose you could say we had resigned ourselves to the situation.

Meanwhile, the crops came in. Even in the best years, some of our tomatoes would have bad spots on them. We usually didn't eat those. I would toss them into the compost pile and take only the best vegetables up to the house.

But one day, for no particular reason, I tossed one of the bad tomatoes outside the garden fence, hurling it toward the groundhog hole. I watched with a bit of satisfaction as it dropped down the hole and disappeared. I tossed more tomatoes. Soon the mouth of the hole was choked with ripe red vegetables.

After a while, this became a daily ritual for me. I would separate the bad vegetables and toss them into the hole, sometimes filling the entrance.

It was about then that the nightly raids on the garden mysteriously stopped. Why, after a summer of skirmishes, would the groundhog declare a truce?

When I mentioned it to my grandfather, a strange light came into his eyes.

"Let's go up to that hole," he said.

We sat on the ground at the entrance to the hole.

"Robin," Grandpa said, "I should have thought of this sooner. Here we were, making war on this groundhog, when we never even stopped to reason with him. I should be ashamed, calling myself a woodsman and a nature lover and here I was, acting like someone who doesn't know the first thing about wild animals."

Then my grandfather spoke into the hole. "Groundhog," he said respectfully, "I know you're down there."

A faint, irritating buzz came from the hole. I guess the batteries were getting low.

"I know you're down there," my grandfather repeated, "and I know we have been at war all summer. But I have come to make an agreement. If you will stay out of the garden from here on, I will make sure that we bring all of our damaged vegetables up here to your hole. You'll have delivery right to your door. What do you say?"

A faint buzzing came from the hole.

I don't know if the groundhog heard or understood my grandfather.

But I do know that from that day on, no groundhog ever attempted to raid our garden again. And from what I could see, that groundhog hole was in use for many years after, and it may still be today.

I like to think the groundhog did hear us. And sometimes I think about the great-great descendants of the old groundhog. I wonder how they must feel, lying down there in their burrow, staring at the rusted hulk of the Tunnel Tickler. Maybe they see it as an artifact from another time. Maybe they view it as we would a marooned spacecraft, a mysterious bit of technology from an alien species. Maybe they tell stories and sing groundhog songs about it.

But through the years my grandfather kept his promise. And so did the groundhogs.

The Groundhog War was over.

The Silver Lake Trout

Grandpa was a dedicated fisherman. Sometimes my grandmother said he was too dedicated. In the summers he never missed a day of fishing and, once I got the hang of it, neither did I. We usually fished the mountain streams. Or we would climb in the pickup and ride over to Silver Lake, a liquid jewel of water that lay, spangling in the sunlight, just down the road from Grandpa's house.

One day while we were at the lake, a

strange thing happened. It started out as a regular morning of fishing—and then I caught a great big three-pound lake trout. I pulled him into the boat and was working the hook out of the lower jaw when I made the mistake of looking him in the eye.

What I saw was a gleam of intelligence. I could have sworn that he winked at me.

I said, "Grandpa, look at this."

My grandfather put down his rod and took the fish from me, looking him over. The fish fixed his eye on my grandfather.

"This is one of them smart ones," my grandfather said. "We'll save him and keep him for a pet."

"A pet fish?" I asked.

My grandfather nodded. "Your uncle Jimmy caught one here years ago, back before you were born. Jimmy brought that fish up on the land with him and taught him to do tricks like a dog."

"Naw," I said, "that's just a story..."

Grandpa shook his head. "No, it's not, and I can prove it. If Jimmy could do it, I can, too. We'll start tonight."

He slipped the trout into a bucket of clean water and the fish swam around, looking up at me with those intelligent eyes.

Once we were back on land, my grandfather carried the trout around to an old-fashioned rain barrel that sat outside the house, and dumped the fish into the barrel. The fish swam around just fine.

"What did you do that for?" I asked.

"You'll see," Grandpa said slyly.

That night, my grandfather snuck out to that rain barrel with an empty bucket. While the fish was asleep, my grandfather dipped out a bucketful of water and dumped it on the ground.

And every night, after dinner, my grandfather would sneak out to that rain barrel and dip out another bucketful of water.

After about two weeks, that barrel had only a little puddle of water in the bottom.

And that fish had learned to breathe in the air!

I remember the very first morning we took him out of the barrel.

There was a real heavy dew on the grass that morning. My grandfather lifted the fish out and laid him in the dew. That moisture was just enough to keep him alive.

My grandfather got down on his hands and knees in front of the trout. He dangled a worm in front of the fish's nose and motioned with his other hand, all the while saying, "Come here, boy, come to me."

That fish was so intelligent he understood right away what my grandfather wanted. He reached out with his front fins and pulled himself across the slick grass toward my grandfather.

My grandfather dropped the worm into the fish's waiting mouth and smiled. "This is gonna work!" he said.

And it did. My grandfather was able to teach the fish to follow him all over the dewy grass. He taught him to roll over and play dead. He even taught him how to fetch worms. Every morning, while the dew was on the grass, my grandfather would work that fish and exercise him.

It was about then that I had to go away on a family vacation for two weeks—a long time when you're training a fish. When I came back, I was amazed at the progress my grandfather had made.

As soon as our car pulled into my parents' driveway, I leaped out and ran over to my grandfather's. I saw him coming toward me across his front yard, waving and shouting, "Howdy, old-timer!"

And there beside my grandfather, balanced on his hind fins, was the fish, walking along like a human being!

Everyone was amazed.

"How did you do it?" I asked.

"Oh," Grandpa said modestly, "it just took a little training."

That fish looked up at me and winked.

After that, that fish could go anywhere with us.

Every evening we'd walk around the lake together, and every night he slept peacefully in the barrel. We never included him in any of our fishing trips; we didn't think he'd see the point. The lazy days of summer passed like a dream.

Then one day a terrible thing happened.

We were out enjoying our evening stroll around the lake when we wandered out onto an old wooden boat dock to get a better view of the sunset. The fish slipped in a puddle of water and fell into the lake.

For a moment, my grandfather and I were too stunned to react.

My grandfather grabbed my arm as we watched that fish sink like a rock.

"Quick," Grandpa urged me, "jump in and get him or he'll drown."

It was a tense moment. I pulled off my sneakers and jumped into the water feet first. The water was clear and deep. Three, four strokes took me down into the cold, watery depths. At last I saw the fish, lying on the bottom of the lake, his body twisting in agony.

I swam down and cradled him to me, bursting up to the surface just as my breath ran out.

My grandfather took the limp fish from me and laid him on the dock. Then he hauled me up out of the water. I shook and shivered like a dog as we watched that poor fish lying still on the dock.

"He's swallowed a lot of water," Grandpa said.

Then my grandfather did an amazing thing. He got down on his hands and knees and began to give the fish mouth-to-gill resuscitation.

At first I thought it was hopeless. But slowly the little guy started to come around. Then he coughed and choked up all the water and his gills began working in the air, just as they had all summer.

That evening, we laid the fish back in the bottom of the barrel to rest. He seemed all right, just a little weak from his terrible ordeal.

"I should have known better," my grandfather said later that night. "You just can't go against nature. We never should have taken that fish out of the water. We've got to find a way to get him back again."

So every night, after that fish fell asleep,

my grandfather would sneak out to the rain barrel with a full bucket of water and pour in a little bit.

After about two weeks, the barrel was full and the fish had learned to breathe in the water.

On the last day of my summer vacation, we put the fish in a bucket of water and put the bucket in the boat. We rowed way out into the center of the lake and just sat, listening to the water lap against the sides of the boat.

The sun was dipping down, coloring the sky with streaks of red and purple. At that hour, all the lake is a mirror. I could see everything reflected back to me in the surface of the lake. As I looked down over the side of the boat, I saw my surroundings in the gray, watery mirror.

I saw a vast sky, with white clouds drifting by.

I could see a chevron of wild geese fly over, honking.

I could see the willows that hung their sorrowful arms in the water.

I could see our boat, with my grandfather and me.

And I knew: The summer was over.

I guess my grandfather was thinking the same thing. We just sat there, neither of us wanting to let the fish go, to let the summer go, but we knew we had to.

"Go ahead," my grandfather whispered. "You do it. You're the one who caught him. You're the one who should send him back."

Before I could think too much more about it, I hefted the bucket and dumped that fish overboard. He slipped like an arc of silver into the lake. And that was the last I ever saw of him.

That was one of the last times I saw my grandfather, too. Because he died a little bit after that. The heart attack he had survived earlier in the summer was a warning. But none of us wanted to believe that our time together was coming to an end.

Then one morning in the first cool days of fall, Grandma walked over to our house and said that Grandpa had passed away peacefully in the night.

Things were different after my grandfather was gone.

Now my rambles through the woods and by the water were solitary, filled with memories. No matter where I went, it seemed that every rock and every tree held some special remembrance. Chattering squirrels and falling leaves and thunderstorms all reminded me of him. And, for a while, that made the sadness of his passing seem all the more painful.

Looking back, I suppose my grandfather

would have laughed at me for being so sentimental. Because if there was one thing I had learned, it was that he was as much a part of the woods as an old decaying tree stump, with its crumbling wood turning back into soil.

And as long as there are fish swimming or eagles flying or black bears making their way through the mountain crags, as long as there are elderberries and hickory nuts and mayapples, as long as the seven mountain ranges lie purple and misty in the evening light, my grandfather's spirit will be there, for anyone to see and touch.

And that's a true story.